Goodnight to Annie

An Alphabet Lullaby

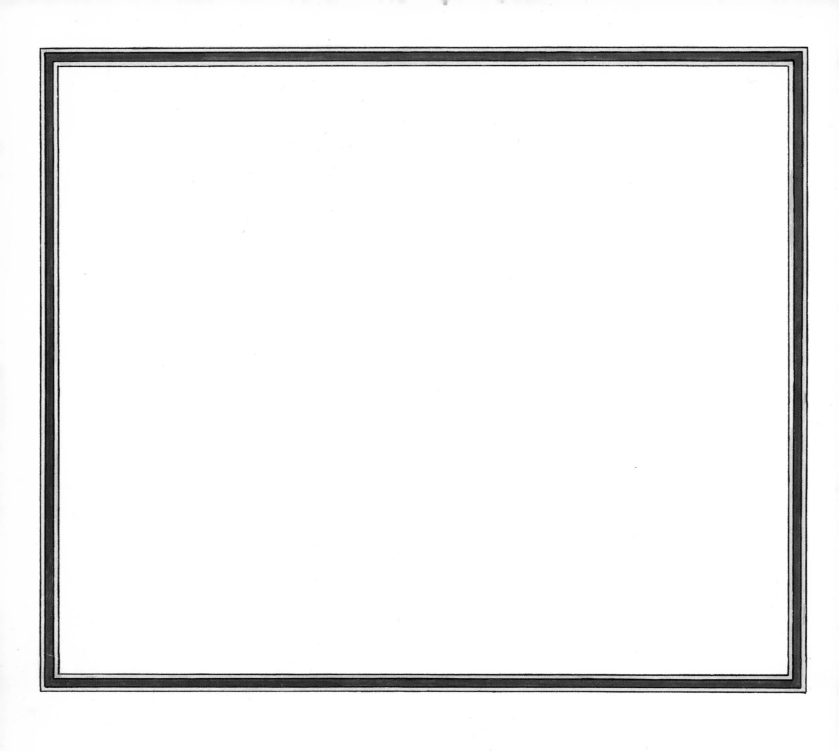

Goodnight to Annie

An Alphabet Lullaby

Eve Merriam

Illustrated by

Carol Schwartz

Hyperion Books for Children

For my dear, dear sister, Del.
— E.M.

For my mother and father, John and Mary Mullenix.
— C.S.

For more information address Hyperion Books for Children, 114 Fifth Avenue, New York, New York 10011.
FIRST EDITION
1 3 5 7 9 10 8 6 4 2

Library of Congress Cataloging-in-Publication Data
Merriam, Eve.   Goodnight to Annie / Eve Merriam; illustrated by Carol Schwartz.   p.   cm.
Summary: In alphabetical order, creatures all over the world fall asleep, from alligators
dozing in the mud to zebras asleep on their sides.
ISBN 1-56282-205-5 (trade) — ISBN 1-56282-206-3 (lib. bdg.)
[1. Bedtime — Fiction.   2. Animals — Fiction.   3. Alphabet.]   I. Schwartz, Carol, ill.   II. Title
PZ7.M543Go 1992   [E] — dc20   92-7111   CIP   AC

The artwork for each picture is prepared in gouache with colored pencil and ink.
This book is set in 24-point Schneidler.

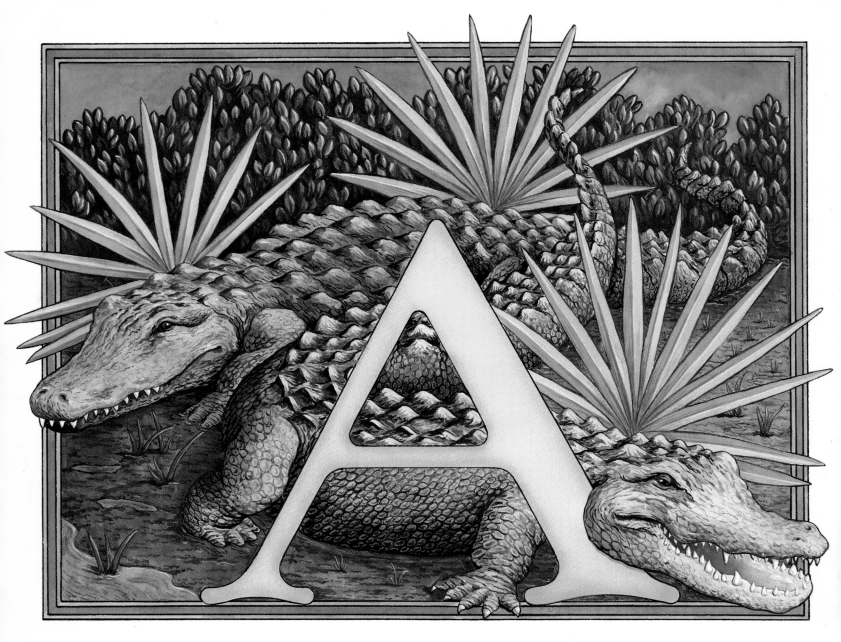

Alligators are dozing in the warm mud.

Bees are clinging to their sweet honey hive.

Cats are closing in their claws.

Dogs are dreaming of digging up juicy bones.

Elephants are curling in their trunks.

Fireflies flicker and glow like tiny flashlights
in the field of darkness.

Grass is silently growing.

Horses are leaning on pillows
of fresh-scented hay in the barn.

Inchworms are inching, minching along.

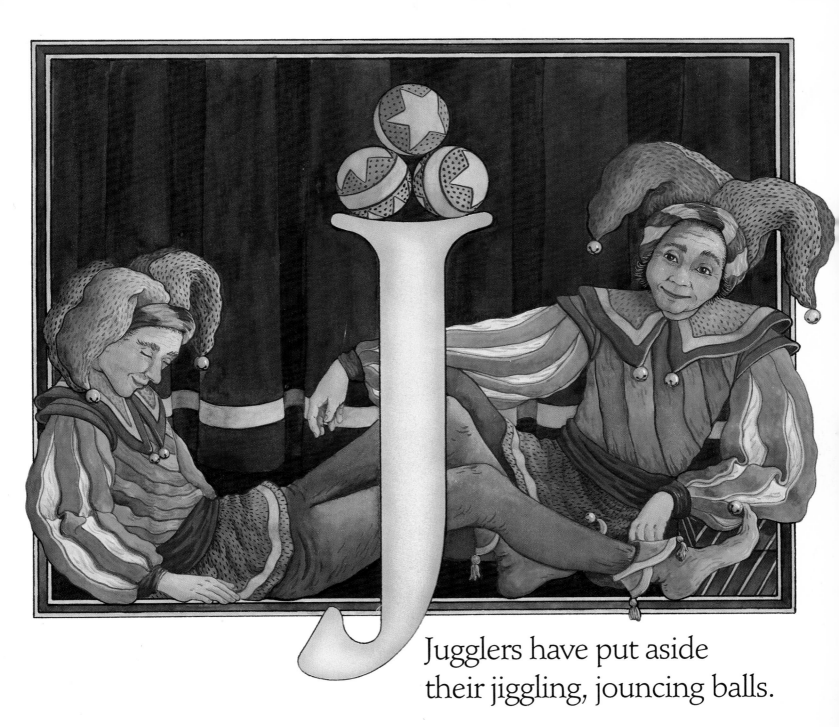

Jugglers have put aside
their jiggling, jouncing balls.

Kittiwakes can hardly keep awake to call,
"Kittiwake, kittiwake, kittiwake, kittiwake."

Llamas are lying down in wooly pajamas.

Mice are munching the quiet holes in cheese.

Nightingales are nodding in their nest.

Oysters are in their oyster beds.

Penguins are folding in their flippers.

Queens are doffing their crowns and drowsing under downy quilts.

Rainbows are fading from their rush of bright colors
to rose and russet and deep indigo.

Star-shaped snowflakes are drifting,
sifting soundlessly to the ground.

Turtles are tucking in their turtle necks.

Umbrella trees are spreading their glossy dark leaves.

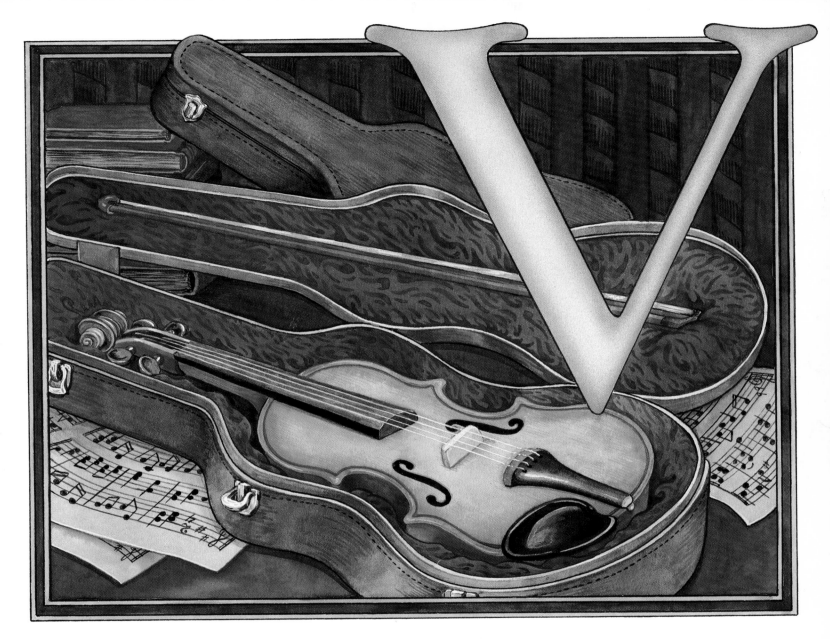

Violins are enclosed in velvet-lined cases.

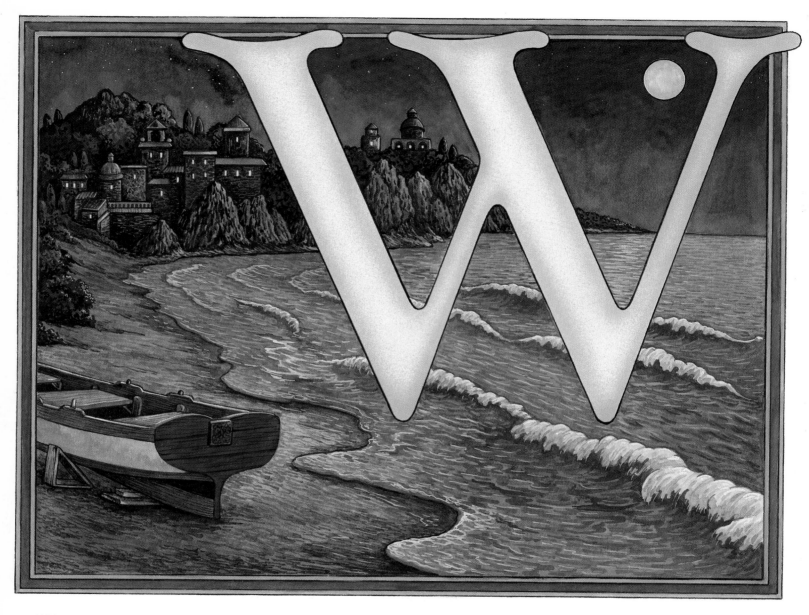

Waves wash over the shore with a hush, shush, shhh....

Xebecs are slowly sailing in the Mediterranean mist.

Yodelers on mountaintops have stopped yodeling,
"Yo-lee-oh-lay-lee-ho,
yo-lee-oh-lay-lee-oh," and are yawning.

Zebras are already asleep on their striped sides
in the zzzzzzzzzzzzzzzzzzoo.